This book is dedicated to every brilliant brother and sister on the planet of African descent. You are the spirit of God seeking to manifest itself in this space and time. You are your ancestors returned. You are worthy of praise and love. Be brilliant and always be seen in a brilliant light.

Copyright 2020 by Kevin Rakeen White All rights reserved.

Written by Kevin Rakeen White.

Illustrated by Keith Williams.

No part of this book may be copied, reprinted, or reproduced by any means without the expressed written permission of the publisher. Limited excerpts are permitted in reviews or in brief references with attribution.

My alarm clock called me to attention. As I rolled out of bed to the floor, trying to reach the alarm clock, my nose started twitching. The aroma was strong. Before long, I was running downstairs to see what was going on.

Momma was in the kitchen seasoning fresh vegetables and BBQ chicken, G-Ma was making her homestyle sweet tea and lemonade, and G-Ma-Ma was overseeing the whole process. By this time, I was thinking to myself, "What in the world am I missing?"

Everyone was smiling and profiling, so I put on a smile too, walking slowly through the house thinking, "What would my dad do?" I ran to the living room to get to the front door, but I backtracked when I saw my sisters playing on the floor. They were happier than normal.

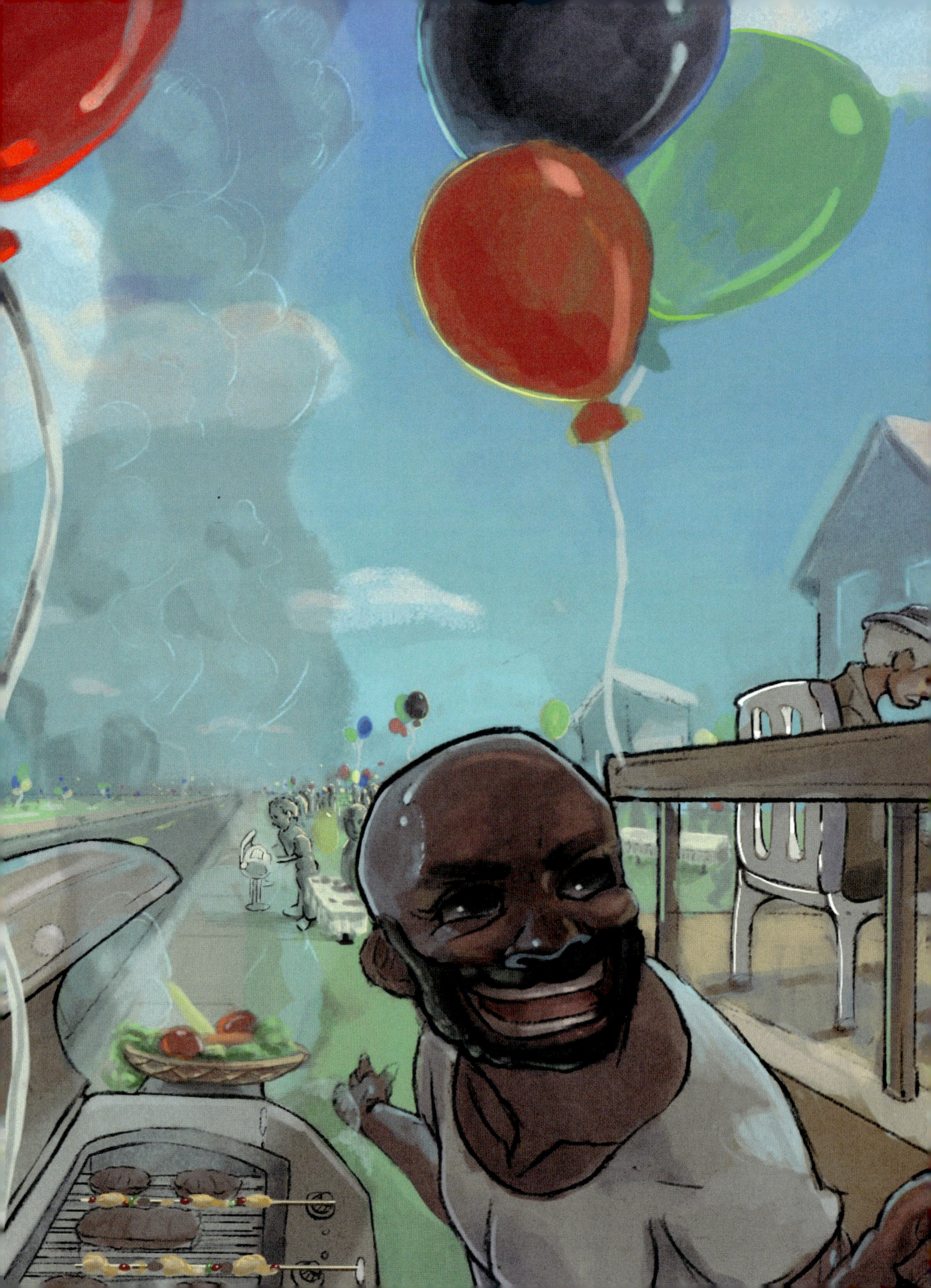

The great aroma grew as I flew straight to the front door. I opened the screen, and Daddy was there, grilling up a storm. My grandfather and great-grandfather were playing chess. When I saw all the grills and people on the block, I knew I had overslept. It was the day of the block party! Now it all made sense! With my nose twitching and my stomach rumbling, I was ready.

Momma stormed from the kitchen with a tin pan in her hand. I could tell the pot was hot because she was screaming, "Boy, move!" So I ran. It was a beautiful day and I was just getting started. I ran up to my room to get dressed for the block party. I couldn't wait to hear the story that G-Pop-Pop was going to share in the elder circle. Every elder gets a turn, but my G-Pop-Pop's stories are just a bit more personal.

I went to the bathroom, turned on the radio, and dropped in my CD. The sound was jumping, Lupe Fiasco's "All Black Everything" is how my mornings begin. With the shower running and the mirror fogging, I was singing along. I love being a brilliant African-American man, powerful and strong. I was made for a time like this. With this much love and support, nothing could go wrong.

Out of the shower, I grabbed my black shorts and a black tee with a v-neck, then took my green-and-red African medallion and placed it around my neck. Looking in the full-body mirror behind my bedroom door, checking my militant swag, I thought to myself, "I look just like my dad."

Before going back downstairs, I chanted my affirmation, "Always remember you have one mouth and two ears. You are brilliant and bright. Just listen to everything around you and stay in your light. Words are sacred, so watch what you say, have fun, remain loyal, and have a great day."

The block was hot and smelling great. Children were playing with hula hoops and skating with inline skates. I stood on the steps before I made my move. The scene was like a dream; in other words, it was beautiful.

Mr. and Mrs. Love are the oldest of all the elders on the block, so everyone must consult with them before anything—move, pause, or stop. They are the king and queen of our block; just like in an African village, they have the power to let all power go. In other words, they can cool things down quickly if they get too hot.

My next stop was down the block for a game of half-ball, or to the court to play some rock. On my way, I saw Mr. and Mrs. White teaching their son how to ride his first bike. Mr. and Mrs. Ali were cooking up a storm as well, and their daughters were running a garage sale. The Alis are the largest family on the block. They have thirteen boys, two daughters, and a nephew they've adopted. Mrs. Ali's heart is the size of Mount Everest, so every time we have a block party, she makes it that much better.

The Smiths are talented and gifted in every sense of the word, and their daughter Phoenix loves to feed the neighborhood birds. The Waller family house stays jumping like Jax; it's where everybody in the neighborhood can eat if they don't have money, without having to worry about paybacks. We call it Johnnie's Place, and it's filled with love, happiness, and lots of grace. I love my block.

"Hey all! I'm ready to play, y'all, so bring out the stick and half-ball! This time I got first, Ade." I was excited to play half-ball.

"Say no more; I'm ready to beat you bad. After I beat the breaks off you, you can run back up the block to go cry to your dad," Ade said jokingly.

Zion cracked a smile. Ade pitched the half tennis ball and I swung that broomstick like there was no tomorrow.

"Catch it!" Ade shouted.

"There's no catching that, buddy!" I said, laughing at his facial expressions.

The game was going great, and getting better as the day went on. After we played half-ball, we got in about an hour of soccer and basketball. I was still waiting for Brilliant Bobby and a few others to come through before going to the elder circle.

"Here comes Dr. Imani and her family," Ade said, as he pointed in our teacher's direction.

"Where?" I asked, trying not to show my excitement.

"Guess who's with her, Militant Mike?" Zion asked, giggling.

"Don't tell me," I said. "Is it who I think it is?"

"Turn around, crazy, and see for yourself," Zion exclaimed.

As soon as I turned around, Dr. Imani and her family were about five steps from us.

"How are you, Dr. Imani?" we all said in unison.

"Hey boys, how's it going? Looking good out here," Dr. Imani replied joyfully.

"It is looking good out here, Dr. Imani," I said while looking at her oldest daughter, Miesha, even though she's ten years older than me.

"Okay, boys. Is your mother up the street, Militant Mike?" Dr. Imani asked.

"Yes," I said, smiling at Miesha.

"Okay. We will see you all when you come up the block," Dr. Imani said.

"Where are you going, Miesha?" I asked excitedly.

"To your house," she replied. "Are you coming up?"

"In just a minute, lovely," I replied. "Hey, Miesha, you know I will be eleven this year...and nine years after that I will be twenty," I said, smiling.

Miesha smiled at me. I believe I made her day.

"Here's Bobby," Zion shouted. Everyone gave out handshakes and daps. We raced up the block to the house to get some food, just before the elder circle.

"The last one to the house is a rotten egg!" Ade shouted.

With the wind under our feet, great-smelling food in the air, and music ringing in our ears, we were ready to throw down.

Zion was the first to reach the house, and Sleepy was the rotten egg. Before we could get our food, we had to let Mr. and Mrs. Love get served first. After that, we were able to get our eat on. The children ate in one circle and the elders ate in another.

After everyone was done with their food, we came together to hear the stories during the elder circle. The elder circle was so large that our circle was in the middle of theirs during storytime, which is also known as a Sankofa moment.

The Loves told the first story, one about a pianist who changed the game completely—Scott Joplin, a man of great talent and skill. Jahmere was elated when he heard about Mr. Joplin, but a sad cloud came over him when he learned about the treatment of Mr. Joplin and others like him—whose great talent was used for the good of others, and who didn't receive proper recognition until later in life. Next, Dr. Imani told many short tales in a very big way. I loved every moment of it.

It was now G-Pop-Pop's time to tell us a story. His stories always felt real—and when I say real, I mean real. G-Pop-Pop is the shortest of the elders, but a powerful man. He carries a staff twice his size, with faces engraved in it. G-Pop-Pop said the spirit world walks with him while he's here, and his staff creates openings for dialogue from ancient times and times that have yet to arrive.

He's the last living blueprint for all the men in my family; that's why storytime is so important to our block parties. Storytime is also a time to catch up on our story as a people—ancient, modern, and otherwise. We've come to know all the families on the block through the stories from their eldest family members.

G-Pop-Pop rose to his feet, and all the talking stopped as soon as his staff touched the earth. We all sat in amazement while G-Pop-Pop went into a trance to gather memories from the past. I love my G-Pop-Pop. When he opened his eyes, a gentle storm was born, from his eyes to the earth. G-Pop-Pop started chanting faster and faster as his staff started drawing words in the grass.

The next thing we knew, G-Pop-Pop was back with a story to tell. "Ashe, I hear you," G-Pop-Pop said quietly, as if returning with dialogue from the past.

"Milam, the bigger of the two, carried a flashlight in one hand and an army-issue .45 pistol in the other. The brothers walked through the screened front porch of the cotton-field shack and stopped at the door, ready for action," he explained. "All this because a white woman said this young child whistled at her," G-Pop-Pop concluded as his staff backtracked through the writing in the earth to release what he had written. G-Pop-Pop gave so much during his story that he had to take a seat immediately after.

Looking at the faces in the circle, I could see that everyone wanted more. It felt like G-Pop-Pop hadn't given us the entire story.

"So, did the men ever find the boy that night?" Tij asked.

"Not only did they find him, sweetie, but a young child from Chicago died that night and never saw his family again," G-Pop-Pop explained passionately.

"Why would someone do that to a child for whistling?" Saida cried.

"The world was a different place in those days," G-Pop-Pop said. "The woman even admitted later that she made the whole thing up."

"What was his name?" Aquae asked.

"Emmett Till," G-Pop-Pop replied.

G-Pop-Pop's story made me think long and hard about some of the choices we make.

Daddy said it's important to always be aware of our surroundings. "Always know where you are when you are, and move strategically," he said before going to get another plate.

"What do you think Daddy meant by that?" I asked Brilliant Bobby.

"I'm not sure," Brilliant Bobby replied, "but I think we'll get it in time."

"Who's up for some more water ice and pretzels?" I shouted out to all my friends. "Raise your hands!"

Everyone's hands took flight above their heads. We all rushed over to Mr. and Mrs. Brown's side of the block to get some of their fresh homemade treats. We only had ten minutes before Mr. and Mrs. Smith were going to start karaoke in front of their house, just before the special guest appeared for the final block party presentation.

Before the final presentation, I went over to my house to grab a shrimp kabob with a small bottle of water. Just before I headed over to the Jones' house, I stood on the top step, thinking, "I love it when we have block parties. Our block captain is the best; Sonya's her name and unity is her game. There's so much love in the air, and so many faces filled with joy and laughter."

My grandfather and great-grandfather were still playing chess, and G-Ma-Ma and G-Ma were sitting in their rocking chairs, showing my sisters and their friends how to sew and knit. Daddy and Momma were standing by the side of the grill, watching all of this.

Mr. Pascal, the founder and CEO of Dexia Media, was the man behind the camera. He looks like the rapper Special Ed, and he's a magnificent photographer. His images can bring a dead man to life, as the elders tell it. And it was about that time!

Brother P, as he likes to be called, stood on stage to announce the final presentation of the day. "If you can hear the sound of my voice, clap once!" he said, but some people were still deep into the festivities. So he raised his tone, "If you can hear the sound of my voice, clap twice!" All became silent. He gave direction for the order of the picture. The elders sat in chairs in a half-circle. The children sat at their feet, and the adults stood around us. "Say 'block party!'" Brother P said as the flash from his camera illuminated the moment.

I AM...

NAME: Michael Mosiah Massy

NICKNAME: Militant Mike

SPIRIT: Marcus Mosiah Garvey

AGE: 10

RACE: African-American

GRADE: 5th

DREAMS: To be a great leader and work to better the living conditions of Africans at home and abroad.

HOBBIES: Studying the works of historical figures, playing soccer, listening to hip-hop, watching documentaries, going to poetry lounges, debating, volunteering at homeless shelters and other places that can benefit from his service, and reading and writing poetry.

DIET: Omnivore

FAMILY: Both parents, both sets of grandparents, both sets of great-grandparents, godparents, two younger sisters, an uncle on his father's side, three aunts and two uncles on his mother's side.

Introduce Yourself

NAME:
NICKNAME:
SPIRIT:
AGE:
RACE:
GRADE:
DREAMS:
HOBBIES:
DIET:
FAMILY:

ABOUT THE SPIRIT OF MILITANT MIKE

Social activist Marcus Mosiah Garvey Jr. was born August 17, 1887, in St. Ann's Bay, Jamaica. Self-educated, Garvey founded the Universal Negro Improvement Association, dedicated to promoting African-Americans and resettlement in Africa. In the United States, he launched several businesses to promote a separate black nation. After he was convicted of mail fraud and deported back to Jamaica, he continued his work for black repatriation to Africa.

Marcus Mosiah Garvey was the last of eleven children born to Marcus Garvey Sr. and Sarah Jane Richards. His father was a stonemason, and his mother was a domestic worker and farmer. His father was a great influence on Marcus, who once described him as "severe, firm, determined, bold, and strong, refusing to yield even to superior forces if he believed he was right." His father was known to have a large library, where young Garvey learned to read.

At age fourteen, Marcus became a printer's apprentice. In 1903, he traveled to Kingston, Jamaica, and soon became involved in union activities. In 1907, he took part in an unsuccessful printers' strike, and the experience kindled his passion for political activism. Three years later, he traveled throughout Central America working as a newspaper editor and writing about the exploitation of migrant workers in the plantations. He later traveled to London, where he attended Birkbeck College (University of London) and worked for the *African Times and Orient Review*, which advocated pan-African nationalism.

Brilliant Bobby and the Kids of Karma
Block Party

Lesson at a Glance

Summary: Militant Mike can't wait for his neighborhood block party to get started. On a beautiful day, he eagerly awaits the love and support that the people in his community display for one another. He also looks forward to wonderful storytelling by the elders, which will enable him to take a glimpse into history.

Skills:
  Comprehension Skill: Fact or Opinion
  Vocabulary: adopted, aroma, elated, medallion, omnivore, overseeing, sacred, strategically, unison
  Comprehension Strategy: Summarize
  Language Focus: Adjectives
  Literary Focus: Plot — Beginning, Middle, End
  Fluency: Change Voice, Characters

Before Reading

Building Background — Access Prior Knowledge: Display the cover and read the title. Have the students describe a block party and ask them if they've ever been to one. Ask: "What kinds of activities might take place at a block party?"

Set a Purpose: Have volunteers identify some of the food that may be at the block party. Then have partners go through the book to set a purpose for reading, such as: "I will read to find out about the characters and their roles in the community."

More Pre-Reading Activities

Comprehension Skill — Fact or Opinion: Preview the comprehension skill with students. Say: "A fact is something that is true and is supported by evidence. An opinion is something you believe or feel to be true, which is open to debate."

Have students flip through pages 1–7, noting the events taking place in Militant Mike's house and on his block. Help students distinguish between fact and opinion as you point out several actions.

Vocabulary: Introduce the vocabulary words using individual white boards, chart paper, or any other type of visual aid. Have students identify words they already know. Then discuss the words and their meanings. Ask questions such as the following, and have students explain their reasoning:

When might you smell a pleasant **aroma**? When your favorite meal is being cooked, or when the trash truck drives by?

When might you be **elated**? When you get a paper cut, or a brand-new puppy?

Who would you consider to be an **omnivore**? A person who eats only vegetables, or a person who loves steak?

Which of the following people needs **overseeing**? A three-year-old cleaning a mess, or a third-grader tying his or her shoe?

Which of the following is not considered a **sacred** place? A church, a mosque, or a public park?

During Reading

Read the Story. Distribute the "Read the Story" worksheet. Review the directions and questions. Then have students read *Block Party*. They may read the story independently, or you can guide the reading using these prompts.

Page 1: What does it mean to have your alarm clock "call you to attention?"

Page 6: While chanting his affirmation, why does Mike say he has two ears and one mouth?

Page 11: Why might Mike be excited to see Dr. Imani and her family?

Page 16: What made G-Pop-Pop's stories feel real?

More During Reading Activities

Comprehension Strategy Mini Lesson — Summarize:

Explain the strategy: Active readers summarize as they read. Summarizing is a way of briefly retelling what is most important in a text, using your own words. What we consider important in a text depends on our purpose for reading it, and determining what is important often requires us to evaluate that purpose.

How do I do it? As you read, or at the end of a section, stop to recall important information or identify the answer to the question you had before you began reading. Try to distinguish what is important from what is an interesting, but significant, detail.

Read page 2 aloud. Model the strategy. Say: "When I read the description of Momma seasoning fresh vegetables and BBQ chicken, I think of a question I may have had before reading: 'What type of food will they have at the block party?'"

As you guide the reading, pause for students to note important information they will use later to summarize what they've read.

Language Focus Mini Lesson — Adjectives:

Write the words **"easy,"** **"easier,"** and **"easiest"** on the board and read them aloud.

Say: "An adjective describes a person, a place, or a thing. The word **easy** is an adjective."

Circle the –er ending on **easier**. Say: "**Easier** is also an adjective. The **–er** endings shows that two things are being compared." Note that the final "y" in easy was changed to "i" before adding the –er.

Repeat with **easiest** and the –est ending to compare three or more things. Explain that adjectives of two or more syllables often use the words "more" and "most" to make comparisons.

Distribute the "Describe It" worksheet. Ask students to look for adjectives that compare as they reread the story.

ELL: English-Language Learners: Language Transfer

Comparative adjectives may present challenges for native speakers of languages such as Hmong, Korean, and Spanish. In these languages, adjectives do not change form. Comparisons are expressed with the equivalent of more and most in English. Students may say their family is "more big" instead of their family is "bigger." Help students practice comparing with adjectives by correctly restating sentences and emphasizing the comparative or superlative adjective: "Yes, Mom's lemonade is sweeter than the lemonade at the market. G-Mom's lemonade is the sweetest."

Talk About It: Have students share their answers to the "Think About It" questions in the back of the book.

Sample Answers:
1. He speaks of each family on his block with high regard, etc.
2. The respect the elder was given when he stood, no one spoke and everyone listened; how passionately G-Pop-Pop told his story, etc.
3. Answers will vary.
4. Stories were not that long, but they had a huge impact, etc.
5. Possibly another elder, someone famous, etc.

After Reading

Literary Focus: Plot — Beginning, Middle, and End: Tell the students that every story should have a beginning, middle, and end.

The **beginning** is the first part of the story. It is where the writer captures the reader's attention, either with a great opening line, a detailed description of the character or setting, or a glimpse into the topic, problem, or theme of the story. The beginning will set the mood for the reader (e.g., happy, dark, mysterious, silly, exciting). A good beginning makes you want to read more.

The **middle** is where the bulk of the story rests. It explains the topic, gives important details, and holds the reader's attention. Most importantly, it is where we reach the climax or turning point of the story. If the middle is good, it will get the reader

thinking about how the story is going to end.
The **end** of the story is where they story comes to a close. It is the conclusion and solution to the problem. It is where the character learns a lesson or comes to terms with the events that happened. A good ending will keep the reader thinking about the story long after it is finished. A great ending leaves the reading feeling satisfied.

Comprehension — Fact or Opinion
Distribute the worksheet titled "Fact or Opinion." Have students work with partners to read the statements and decide if each statement is a fact or an opinion.

Vocabulary: Have students create sentences or fictional stories, or retell the story using the vocabulary words from the story.

Fluency: Change Voice, Characters: Tell students that when reading fluently, they need to be able to express themselves readily and effortlessly. When they are reading a story with many characters, this means that they need to place themselves in the mind of each character as they read. Model by reading page 10.

Writing: Possible writing prompts:
1. Have students write a summary of the story, using their own words.
2. Have students create sentences or stories using comparative and superlative adjectives found in the story.
3. Explain the importance of listening to the elders' stories.

Talk About It:
1. What are some examples of how Militant Mike loves the community in which he lives?
2. What did you observe when reading pages 17–21?
3. Do you think there was a reason why the children ate in one circle and the elders ate in another? Why or why not?
4. Explain the following: "Dr. Imani told many short tales in a very big way."
5. Page 22 mentions a special guest who will appear for the final block party presentation. Who do you think that will be?

Glossary of Terms

Adopt – To take a child of other parents legally as your own child.
Aroma – A noticeable, and usually pleasant, smell.
Elated - Very happy and excited.
Medallion – A decoration shaped like a large medal.
Omnivore – A person or other animal that eats both plants and meat.
Overseeing – To watch and direct work in order to be sure that a job is done correctly.
Sacred – Entitled to reverence or respect.
Strategically – Of or relating to a general plan that is created to achieve a goal.
Unison – Action or speech taking place at the same time.

Aligned to the following **Common Core Standards:**
(www.pdesas.org)

1.1.3.D: Demonstrate comprehension/understanding before reading, during reading, and after reading on grade level texts through strategies such as retelling, summarizing, note taking, connecting to prior knowledge, supporting assertions about text with evidence from text, and non-linguistic representations.

R3.A.1.1: Identify and interpret the meaning of vocabulary.

CC.1.1.3.E: Read with accuracy and fluency to support comprehension: Read on-Level text with purpose and understanding. Read on-level text orally with accuracy, appropriate rate, and expression on successive readings. Use context to confirm or self-correct word recognition and understanding, rereading as necessary.

E03.B-K.1.1.1: Answer questions to demonstrate understanding of a text, referring explicitly to the text as the basis for the answers.

E04.B-K.1.1.1: Refer to details and examples in a text when explaining what the text says explicitly and when drawing inferences from the text.

E04.A-K.1.1.1: Ask and answer questions to demonstrate understanding of a text, referring explicitly to the text as the basis for the answers.

Name_____

Fact or Opinion?

A <u>fact</u> is something that is true and is **supported by evidence**. An <u>opinion</u> is something **you believe or feel to be true, which is open to debate**. Read each statement and decide if it is a fact or an opinion.

Fresh vegetables are the greatest-tasting food of all time.		
The aroma on Militant Mike's block during the day of the block party is the best aroma ever.		
Mr. and Mrs. Love are the oldest of all the elders on the block.		
The Alis are the largest family on the block.		
The Smiths are talented and gifted in every sense of the word.		
Miesha is the most beautiful girl in the world.		
Scott Joplin died on April 1, 1917.		
Emmett Louis Till was murdered for whistling at a white woman.		

Name_____

Read the Story
Read the assigned pages and answer the assigned questions.

Page 2   1. Why is G-Ma overseeing the whole process while in the kitchen?
_____
_____
_____

Page 7   2. Why do you think this scene is like a dream for Militant Mike?
_____
_____
_____

Page 12   3. What can you infer from Mike's comment to Miesha about his age?
_____
_____
_____

Page 15   4. How would you clarify the meaning of the phrase "proper recognition?"
_____
_____
_____

Page 21   5. Elaborate on the statement, "Always know where you are when you are, and move strategically."
_____
_____
_____

Name_____

Describe it!

An **adjective** describes a person, place, or thing. For many words, you can compare two things by adding –er to the adjective, or by using the word **more**. To compare three or more things, you can add -est to the adjective or use the word **most**.

One	Two (Comparative)	Three (Superlative)
sweet	sweeter	sweetest
thin	thinner	thinnest
exciting	more exciting	most exciting

Write the comparative and superlative forms of each adjective. Then use the adjective in a sentence to compare two things or three or more things.

                Comparative   Superlative

1. great   _____   _____

2. large   _____   _____

3. small   _____   _____

4. sacred   _____   _____

Made in the USA
Middletown, DE
10 August 2022